Ruby and the Booker Boys

Brand-new School, Brave New Ruby

Brand-new School, Brave New Ruby

by Derrick Barnes

illustrated by Vanessa Brantley Newton

SCHOLASTIC INC.

New York Toronto London Auckland Sydney
Mexico City New Delhi Hong Kong Buenos Aires

Extra special thanks to Andrea Pinkney and Regina Brooks. Thanks for not giving up on me, Ruby, and her beautiful family.

ISBN-13: 978-0-545-01760-2 ISBN-10: 0-545-01760-2

Library of Congress Cataloging-in-Publication Data Available

20 19 18 17 17/0

Printed in the U.S.A. 40
First printing, July 2008

To Kamryn & Jaloni Crayton—

Living, breathing Ruby Bookers to the core

☆ Chapters ☆

☆ Ruby's Laptop Journal ☆

1
Rise, Shimmy, and Shine

I woke up at 7:15 in the morning.

The first day of school was *really* real when my clock radio went off at 7:30. Ma had fixed it the night before to play my favorite song, "Cotton Candy Clouds," a let's-get-going-and-have-a-good-first-day-of-school song.

The coolest group in the world, the Crazy Cutie Crew, sings that song. They only have three members. But I like to pretend I'm the fourth.

As soon as the first note hit my ears, I stood up on my bed like it was a stage (even though Ma doesn't like me to). I sang every single word, really loud, as if the Crazy Cutie Crew wrote the song for me:

"When the sun hits the clouds
And rainbows kiss the sky,
A sweet wind blows,
And then I know
That today is mine, all mine."

This is pretty much how I begin each morning. I sing so loud, the rest of my family uses *me* as an alarm clock.

I leaped onto the floor and hit a perfect landing on my super-soft rug. It looks

like big piano keys. But instead of the keys being boring black and white, they are purple and orange.

"Cotton Candy Clouds" was bouncing off every wall in my room when I slid over to my window. I pulled back my curtains and got the biggest hug from the sun. Those morning rays covered my face with a color that's hard to find in a crayon box. If happy was a color I guess that's what I would call it.

Before I knew it I heard someone coming down the hall outside my bedroom door.

It was Ma and my three big brothers, Ro, Ty, and Marcellus. When they got to my room, they were all rubbing their eyes and yawning. From the smell of sausages and eggs floating into my room, I could tell that Daddy was downstairs making breakfast.

"We hear you, Ruby. Loud and clear, baby. Loud and clear," Ma said with her big, pretty smile. She picked me up and squeezed me real warm and tight, just like she does every morning.

"Girl, do you know how early it is? Are you part girl, part rooster?" Ro asked angrily. "You sure do crow loudly."

"Yeah, ladybug," my biggest brother, Marcellus, added. He calls me ladybug. I like it. That name fits me, because I'm cute and I like to think that I bring good luck wherever I go. "We all love your singing, Ruby, and we're used to it, but this is extra, extra early."

"What else do you all expect? That's Rube. It's what she does," my third brother, Ty, said with a grin. He took his glasses out of the pocket of his pajama top, popped them on his button nose, and then said, "Good morning, Rube. Sounds like you're ready for school." He always says nice things to me. I love me some Ty.

"Okay, boys, leave your sister alone. Let's get ready and head downstairs for breakfast," Ma said, pointing down the hallway toward the boys' rooms.

"And you, Miss Superstar Third-grader, you said you wanted to pick out your own outfit this morning. So get to it, sister!" Ma poked my belly. She loves tickling me.

As far as my clothes go, orange and purple rule. Before I went to bed, I hung my first-day-of-school outfit over the chair at my desk. It was a brand-new orange-and-purple shirt, a brand-new jean jumper, long orange-and-purple-striped socks, and to top things off, my favorite shoe combination. One orange sneaker and one purple. I couldn't wait to put everything on to show Ma.

After washing up, brushing my teeth, and putting on my purple-and-orange perfection, I grabbed two bracelets. Purple and orange, of course. And I put on my favorite pretend pearl earrings. Then I pressed REPEAT on my radio alarm clock and sang "Cotton Candy Clouds" even louder. I heard Ro screaming from down the hallway, "GIVE US A BREAK, RUBY!"

I love to get on his nerves.

As I looked in the mirror for the last time, I whispered to myself, "Ruby Marigold Booker, you sure are fabulous!" And that's the truth.

To add a final touch to my fabulousness, I reached for the new book bag Ma made me. Ma can work wonders on her sewing machine, and this time she outdid herself. She sewed me a schoolbag in the shape of a guitar. I want to be a rock star when I grow up, so this new book bag was very special to me.

But there was only one problem. I couldn't grab it and go downstairs for breakfast. Lady Love was sitting on my bag and chomping on the straps. I forgot to mention that I have a pet, and not just any pet. Lady Love is my two-year-old, extra-super-spoiled iguana.

There she sat, looking super girlie, wearing her fake diamond leash and hot pink nail polish on her claws. Lady Love is a real diva. I sure love her. That's how she got her name. Lady Love.

I tickled Lady Love's belly and offered her some iguana snack food. That was all it took. She moved off my book bag. I picked it up quickly, took a deep breath, and ran out the door of my bedroom.

When I turned the corner to head toward the stairs, I bumped into Ma.

"Great look, girl. Nobody can make mismatched shoes look as fabulous as you, Ruby." Ma gave me her pretty smile again.

"Do I look okay, Ma? Do I? I'm so ready for school. Third grade, here I come!" I was excited about my first day at a new school, but I don't think I was *really* ready. Deep down inside, my tummy was turning.

Ma said, "Looks like you wore your head scarf to bed. Your hair still looks nice. Good. Your shoes are tied. Pretty bracelets. Your book bag looks full, and it has all of your supplies in it, right?" Ma gave me one last look.

"Yes, Ma. Yes. I gotta get down for breakfast. Don't want to start my first day at Hope Road Academy on an empty tummy."

I hopped on the handrail and was about to slide down the stairs like my brothers always do. But of course Ma stopped me.

"Girl, are you forgetting you have a skirt on?" she said with that look on her face. Everybody knows the look. It says, "You should know better."

I hopped off the banister and yelled out to Daddy and my brothers, "HERE COMES RUBY!"

2
Breakfast Booker-style

"Is Hope Road Academy going to be ready for the Booker sister?" I asked my brothers.

Roosevelt, who I call Ro, and Marcellus were sitting in their usual seats at the breakfast table. Tyner, who we all call Ty, was kneeling up out of his seat. I waved at everyone like only a princess can.

"Ro, turn up the radio and come put these sausages on the table," Daddy said as he stood at the stove with

10

his apron on. The apron is his favorite. On the front it says:

I BRING HOME THE BACON
AND COOK IT

We listen to all kinds of music in our house, but when it's breakfast time, it's *Daddy* time. We all groove to *his* music and enjoy the breakfasts he makes.

Tyner looked up from a piece of paper he was reading and said, "Ruby, I saved a plate with the strawberry topping that I know you like on your waffles."

"Thanks, Ty. Why can't Ro be as nice to me as you are?" I said, looking in Ro's direction. Ro didn't pay me any attention.

He asked Marcellus, "Hey, man, do you want any sausages or not? I'm not your waitress!" But Marcellus didn't hear a word Ro was saying. He was too busy looking at himself on the side of the toaster, like that toaster was his very own mirror. Marcellus is *so* into Marcellus. That's because of the girls at Hope Road Academy who think he's Mr. Cute. Whatever. He's just Marcellus to me. While Marcellus was checking out his hair in the toaster, [illegible] Ro dump all of Marcellus's [illegible]ges onto his own plate. Then h[illegible] snatched two of Marcellus's waffles. Ro is something else. He looked at me and said, "What, Ruby? I'll take your waffles, too."

I stood up from my seat and told him, "I wish you would try." Then I

crossed my arms and waited for him to come over.

As soon as he stepped a foot in my direction, Daddy said, "Ro, sit down and eat! And give your brother back his sausages." Ro did what Daddy said and then sat down and continued to wolf down his own food. Just when he was about to eat the two waffles he'd taken from Marcellus, Daddy added, "And the waffles, Ro. Give them back to your brother." Nobody knows Ro like Daddy.

Marcellus finally finished grooming at the table, looked up, and saw me.

"Hey, ladybug. Are you finally ready for school, or what?"

"I guess so . . . no . . . I *know* so," I said, trying to be calm and cool just like him. I didn't know how to tell Marcellus the truth. I was so scared of going somewhere new. I was hoping it didn't show.

"That's what I like to hear, ladybug," Marcellus said before he took a sip of Daddy's famous mango-orange breakfast juice.

Ro said, "She better be ready. This is not a little kiddie school. This is a *real* school. For big kids. The long hallways and big crowds will eat you up and spit you out if you're not on your toes." Ro stuffed his big mouth with waffles and eggs. His jaws were so full he looked like a hippo face. I was working hard not to listen to Ro. He's always trying to scare me out of something or make me worried.

Usually, it doesn't work, but this morning it kinda did.

Tyner finished reading what looked like a list of classes he would be taking this school year. Did I mention that he is always on top of things when it comes to school? Did I also mention that he is something like a genius? We all do well in school, but Tyner is crazy with it. He even skipped a grade. He's almost ten, but he's in the sixth grade with Ro, who is almost eleven!

"Everybody will love you, Rube. Trust me. Just be your colorful, creative, nice self," Ty told me before he finished his waffles and took his empty plate to the sink. That's how Ty is. Ma never has to tell him to pick that up, clean this up, or wipe that off. Sometimes he makes the rest of us look bad.

Daddy put the dirty dishes in the dishwasher. He came over to me and gave me a big hug and kiss. He doesn't have a mustache, but the hairs

on his chin are really tickly. I laugh every time he hugs me.

"Ruby, I love your hair, baby. Purple and orange really look good against your pretty skin. You look so ready for the third grade," Daddy said to me. "You'll have new friends in no time." That's when I started to think about my old friends, especially Teresa Petticoat, my BFF from Lunar-Bigsby School.

"So, Daddy, did Teresa Petticoat call me this morning?" I asked him with a big triangle piece of waffle hanging from my mouth. This year she would be going to Hope Road for the first time, just like me. The one thing that might take away these jitters in my tummy was if I knew whether Teresa and I would be in the same classroom. But I wouldn't find that out until I got to school. I sure was hoping on my girl T.

"Not this morning, sweetie. She's probably finishing up her first-day-of-school breakfast, just like you. I'm sure you girls will see each other later," Daddy said. I hoped Daddy was right.

Everyone finished eating at the same time. Those strawberry waffles sure hit the spot. Just then, Ma came down the stairs, and we all looked up toward her like she was a queen. She was carrying two bags so she took her time. Ro, Marcellus, and Ty got up from the table and ran over to help her.

I don't know which one is more of a mama's boy. Ro says Ty is, Marcellus says Ro is, and Daddy says they all are. I agree with Daddy. I guess that's a good thing.

We all grabbed our book bags and headed out the door. Ma gave all of us a good-bye kiss. Daddy gave me a good-bye kiss, too, but gave the boys the handshake they like to call "a pound of Booker."

Ma left at the same time we did. Last year, when I went to Lunar-Bigsby School, Ma and I walked together. The boys walked to Hope Road Academy, in the other direction.

This year was different. Ma walked to work down Chill Brook Avenue, toward Forty-seventh Street. My brothers and I went up Chill Brook Avenue toward Fifty-fifth Street. It made me sad to see Ma going off by herself. I was already missing our morning walks together.

When my old school closed down, Ma decided not to teach at any other school in the area. Instead, she opened up a dance studio on Forty-seventh Street and Evers Avenue. She's a super-good dance teacher. And I'm not just saying that because she's my ma. It's the truth.

Daddy owns his own business. It's a store right down on the corner called The Booker Box. It's one of the most popular stores in the neighborhood for CDs, DVDs, and all kinds of video games. He usually doesn't open the store until 9:30 A.M. Today, by the time Daddy opened his store, I'd be in my new classroom with my new classmates, and hopefully with a lot of new friends.

3
Hope Road Reception

We were a block away from the school. I could see everybody standing outside on the blacktop. It looked like a parade of kids. Not a little parade, but the big Thanksgiving Day parade they have in New York City. My old school only went up to the fifth grade. Hope Road Academy started at kindergarten and went all the way to the eighth grade. That means a lot more kids. I looked all over for my friend Teresa, but I didn't see her anywhere.

I started to get really extra-crazy nervous then. I didn't know anyone except for my brothers. Marcellus must have seen the scared look on my face. He put his arm around my shoulders.

"Don't worry, ladybug. Up here at Hope Road, the Booker boys are like superstars. You feel me? I'm not only the king of the seventh grade, I'm king of the whole Hope Road kingdom."

"Man . . . whatever," Ro said with a jealous look on his face.

Marcellus explained how their popularity would help me ease into such a big crowd of kids. "As soon as everybody sees you walking with us and you tell everybody what your last name is, you're in, baby!"

"Yeah, Rube, being a Booker at this school is definitely a good thing," Tyner added.

Ro jumped in, "What Noodles is trying to say is, everybody who is somebody knows who we are. I'll tell you right now — I'm the man up here, Ruby."

He called Ty by his nickname — Noodles. All my brothers have nicknames. Ty is "Ty Noodles," or "Noodles" for short, because he uses

his brain a lot. All the kids on our block call Roosevelt "Ro" or "Ro Rowdy," because he's a prankster and a troublemaker. And Marcellus, we just call him "Big-Time." He thinks the sun shines on him all day long. He's good at playing a lot of instruments and sports, and he gets good grades. Big-Time can get a big head. That's because all the stuff he's good at really *goes* to his head.

Even with my brothers there to back me up, the excitement that I had at home about my new school was gone. When we got to the school grounds, it was like a siren had gone off. Right away, a bunch of kids started running up to my brothers. Kids were surrounding us from all sides.

I didn't see the microphones or cameras, but it felt like my brothers were being interviewed for TV. The questions came faster than baseball pitches.

"Ty Noodles, will you sit next to me in class?"

"Ro Rowdy, what kind of pranks do you have planned this school year?"

"Marcellus? Marcellus? Do you have a girlfriend?"

The questions kept coming, and

HOPE ROAD
10

the circle of kids around my brothers kept getting bigger. Before I knew it, I had been pushed back, away from my brothers. I couldn't even see Noodles, Ro, and Marcellus anymore. I really felt alone then.

Everybody was bigger than me, and I didn't know anyone. There were a couple of kids from our block who I recognized, but they were all older. I wanted to turn around and run home, grab Ma's hand, and go back to my old school. But I couldn't. Tears rushed to my eyes, but I held them all in. One tear got free and rolled down my face, but I wiped it away quickly. As lonely as I was, I still didn't give up hope that my first day could turn out to be good.

Ty had found a way to sneak out of the crowd of Booker fans, and he spotted me.

"Are you okay, Rube? Sorry we lost you," he said.

"I guess I'm okay," I said with my head down.

Suddenly, a loud bell went off for everybody to go inside. As kids passed us, Ro and Marcellus followed their friends. Ty stood by my side.

"Hey, I'll walk you to your classroom. How's that?" Ty asked.

"That sounds nice, Ty." I smiled.

There were lists posted on the wall next to the office telling kids what classrooms they would be in and who our teachers would be. I looked for two names. Mine and Teresa's. Ty saw my name right away. "You're in Pluto-3, and your teacher's name is Miss Fuqua," he said.

"Do you see Teresa Petticoat's name on my class list?" I asked.

Ty shook his head. "Nope."

I bit my bottom lip.

"But don't worry, Rube, Miss Fuqua is really fun. Even though your friend won't be in your class, you have a cool teacher," Ty said. Hearing him say that made the funny feeling in my tummy settle down. I was really missing Teresa, but it was good to know I would have a nice teacher. One thing was for certain. Even though Ty said she was cool, my teacher had a funny name.

"Fuqua? Is it like *few-kway*? That's her real name?" I asked Ty.

"Sure is. Some people call her Miss Fruitcake."

"Fruitcake?" I joked. I just liked saying *fruitcake*.

"Yep, fruitcake." Ty laughed.

"Stop being silly, Rube. Let's get you to class."

We walked down the hallway and then up the stairs to the second floor. All the classrooms in the school were named after planets and other space things. I liked the name Pluto-3. I hoped I would like the kids in my class as much as I liked the name of my classroom.

We stood in front of my classroom door, and I held Ty's hand tight. I didn't want him to leave me.

"Go on in and add some Ruby Booker flavor to that class," Ty said. "I'm sure they're waiting on you, especially Miss

Fruitcake." I laughed a little, let go of Ty's hand, and watched him run down the hallway to his own classroom.

I slowly turned the doorknob and landed quietly on Pluto-3.

4
Landing on Pluto-3

As soon as I stepped into Pluto-3 I loved what I saw. There were bright colors everywhere and lots of cool posters. And Miss Fruitcake had put out games, tons of books, art supplies, computers, and instruments for all of us kids.

Suddenly, I heard someone call out from the back of the room, "Look around, students. I want you to find the desk that has your name on it. That will be your very own property. It'll be

Pluto-3

your little spot on Pluto-3. Welcome to the third grade."

I turned around and saw the teacher, Miss Fuqua. She looked as fun and colorful as her name. She was kinda tall. Her hair was long and

curly, like my hair is after Ma washes it. She had a gazillion beautiful silver bracelets on her wrists. They jingled every time she moved. More than anything else, she seemed nice. She even looked at me and said, "Good morning, Ruby Booker!"

I smiled and answered, "Good morning, Miss Fruit . . . I mean Fuqua." I almost slipped up but I caught myself. She waved at me and then continued to talk to the rest of the class.

"Walk around the room and get familiar with all of the workstations. I hope you like how I set up the room," Miss Fuqua said to the entire class.

I counted fifteen kids, including me, but there were sixteen desks. Everybody seemed so different, and playful, and happy to be in Miss Fuqua's class. I was, too. That funny-tummy feeling slipped away.

And all of a sudden the words to my favorite song, "Cotton Candy Clouds," filled my head and made me feel real good inside. I hummed and hummed and played my guitar book bag like it was a real instrument. A few of the kids in my class looked at me weird, but I couldn't help it. "Cotton Candy Clouds" was my song.

When I got to my desk, there were two boys sitting near me. The seat next to mine was empty. But the boy who sat behind me looked like trouble. He just wouldn't stop giggling. He had bright red hair. The card on his desk said Manny Flemon. He glanced over at me, read the card on my desk, grinned, and said, "Ruby is an old lady's name."

I read his name out loud. "Manny? You're one to talk. What kind of name is Manny? It sounds like the name of a birthday party clown." Manny Flemon lost his funny-looking grin and frowned at me. Then he shut his mouth.

The boy sitting next to Manny was as skinny as a bundle of straws. His skin was the beautiful brown color of the big chocolate heart Daddy bought Ma for Valentine's Day. He had his hands in his lap and sat quietly. I asked him his name because I couldn't see his card. He moved his lips to speak, but I couldn't hear anything.

Manny jumped in. "That's Lionel Crispy, but we all call him Low-Low. You gotta be real close to him to hear what he says," Manny explained. Then Manny jabbed Low-Low in the ribs. That boy still didn't make a peep. He just laughed and then hunched over. The whole time I thought, *This is who Miss Fuqua, or Miss Fruitcake, hooked me up with? I'm trapped with a kid who talks too much and a kid I can't even hear!*

"Take out your markers and crayons, students," Miss Fuqua told the whole class. "I want you to decorate the name cards on your desks." Now "Cotton Candy Clouds" was going off loud in my head. This had to be heaven! Right away I wrote my name and even drew pictures of animals around the

edges. It was the perfect way to Rubify my new desk.

After that, Miss Fuqua asked us to stand up when she called on us. She wanted us to tell the rest of the class our name, our age, something fun about ourselves, and what we would like to be when we grow up. She also wanted to know if we had any siblings who attended Hope Road. Since Miss Fuqua started at the end of the alphabet and my last name begins with the letter *B*, it gave me some time to figure out what to say.

After the first eleven kids spoke, it was finally my turn. I stood up, cleared

MATH

my throat, straightened my skirt, then spoke out clearly for the whole class to hear. "My name is Ruby. I am eight years old. A fun fact about me is that I *love* trivia. I'm the trivia queen. I know lots of facts about lots of things, like what the highest mountain in the world is, why skunks smell, and how rainbows get their colors." I snapped my fingers and stomped my feet because trivia is so fun, and I know I'm good at it. The whole class laughed. I was the first one to say my thing with some flavor. That's the Ruby Booker flavor that Ty Noodles was talking about.

I continued my introduction when the laughs slowed down. "When I grow up, I want to be a ROCK STAR. I've been taking guitar lessons, and I already know how to sing." I held up my guitar book bag for everyone to see. "When I learn how to play a real guitar — watch out!" The class and Miss Fuqua started laughing

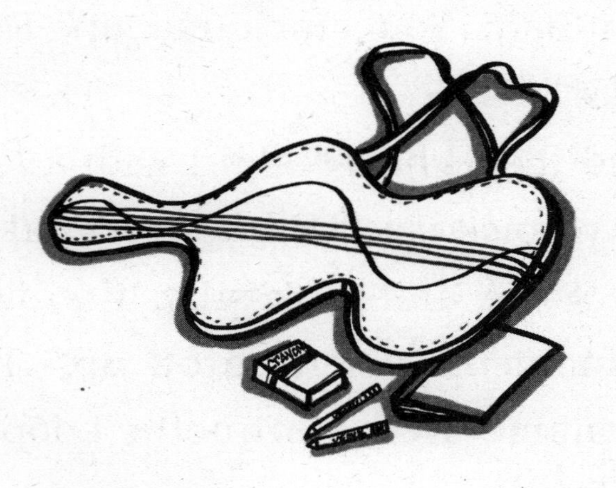

again. I felt like I had the class in the palm of my hand. They started showering me with questions.

I heard one girl say, "Hey, Ruby, my name is Chyna Wentworth. You want to be a rock star? That's so cool!"

Then another girl told me her name. "I'm Mona Sweetroll. I like your hair, your mismatched shoes, and that guitar bag. You crack me up, Ruby Booker!"

And then I heard a girl with a loud, cranky voice say, "Rock stars make a lot of noise and look silly. I want to be a magician when I grow up." That girl's name was Marquetta Loopy. I could see her name card from across the room. Marquetta looked at me and then rolled her eyes. She was the little sister of the Loopy brothers, and from what I heard, nobody likes the Loopy brothers. Marquetta was probably just jealous because my brothers are so popular.

I was upset that Marquetta tried to talk during *my* time. I took a few steps toward her desk, rolled my eyes at her, and said, "Since you want to be a magician, let me see how fast you can disappear. Go ahead. *Poof!* Begone!" The other kids laughed even louder than before.

Miss Fuqua looked at me sternly. Then she gave Marquetta the same look. "Girls, in Pluto-3 we only speak to one another kindly." I nodded to show Miss Fuqua I understood. Marquetta folded her arms. Everyone else was still giggling. Miss Fuqua clapped her hands and said, "Okay, Pluto-3, calm down, calm down!" I started to sit back in my seat when Miss Fuqua said, "Wait, Ruby. Don't forget the sibling part. Do you have any siblings who attend this school?" The whole class looked at me and I couldn't lie. I had to tell the truth.

Right then, I decided to act like Low-Low. I said my brothers' names, but I spoke so softly that no one could hear me. Then I sat down. Bigmouthed Manny yelled out, "What did you say? We couldn't hear you, Ruby."

I stood back up, took a deep sigh, and said, "Yes. I have three big brothers who attend this school. My brothers Tyner and Roosevelt are in the sixth grade, and my brother Marcellus is in the seventh grade." Then I sat back down. For some reason I felt embarrassed because I knew what was about to happen . . . and it did.

Everyone piped up with *ooohs* and *aaahs* and started raising their hands. Then my classmates asked the same questions about my brothers that all the kids had asked in the morning on the playground.

One girl, Gina Crumpy, asked, "So how does it feel being the little sister of the Booker boys?" I wanted to get up and stuff her mouth with notebook paper, but I remembered what Miss Fuqua said about treating one another nicely. How did Gina think it felt to be a Booker? Sometimes it was fun. Other times it was just like being any other girl who had a bunch of big brothers. No biggie.

And just when I had started to really become a hu-gantic fan of Miss Fuqua, she had to put in her two cents. "Marcellus was one of the best students I ever had. I had him in the third grade, and now he's grown up to be such a multitalented, extremely intelligent Hope Road student. You should be proud, Ruby Booker." Miss Fuqua spoke with so much joy in her voice that my tummy started to rumble again. All the attention I'd been getting from my new classmates was being showered on my brothers.

One minute I was feeling good about my new school, and the next I was down.

Then a little miracle happened.

Miss Fuqua asked us all to line up, one at a time, so that we could take a bathroom break before the rest of the students got up to speak. But just then, the door opened and my best, best, best friend of all time walked in the door. There she was — Teresa Petticoat! She saw me and her cheeks got all red. Her strawberry blonde hair was pulled back into a ponytail, with a yellow bandanna to keep it all in place.

And to make the miracle even sweeter, Miss Fuqua put Teresa at the desk right next to me. I'd wondered why that desk had been empty. Now

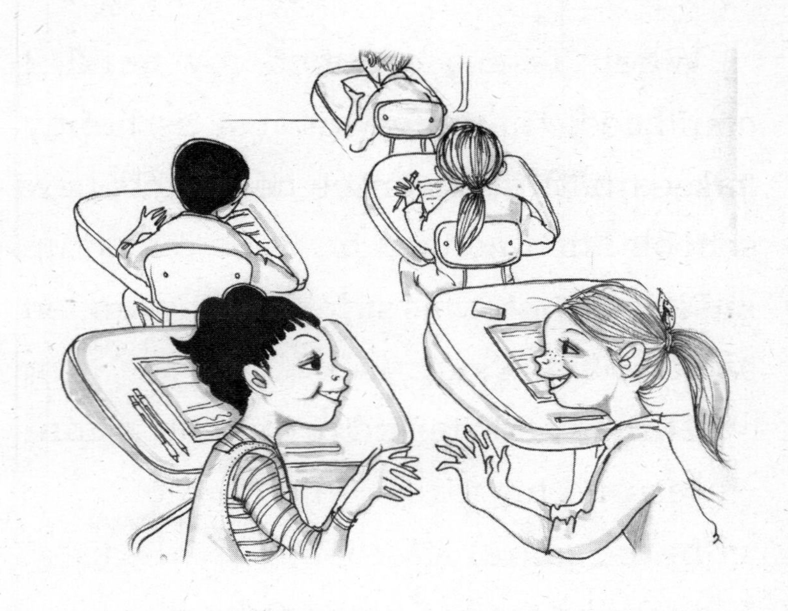

I knew why! Teresa pushed her stuff into the coat closet and then came to sit down near me. We didn't say a word. We just looked at each other and smiled and then did our secret handshake underneath our desks.

When Teresa grabbed my hand, I could feel that she was just as happy to see me as I was to see her in this new school. I had no idea how she ended up in Pluto-3, but I was sure glad she landed safely. What a surprise!

Things had started to look up again.

Me and my girl T.

In the same classroom.

Pluto-3 was the place to be.

5
Ro Rowdy

"T, I thought you would be in the other third-grade class, but here you are with me! I'm so glad to see you," I whispered to Teresa.

"Well, Ruby, I'll tell ya. It seems like they got me mixed up with some gal named Catrina Williboat," Teresa explained. "*She's* in the other third-grade class, and *I'm* supposed to be in here," Teresa whispered back.

Teresa and her family moved onto our block from Memphis, Tennessee, about three years ago. She is soooo country, but I love it. She speaks with the sweetest Southern-girl twang. Her voice is like a piece of peach velvet cake.

Right then, the PA system came on with a loud screech. Everyone put their hands over their ears. Then the principal, Miss Cherrybaum, came slicing through the speakers with an announcement. Miss Fuqua told us all to be quiet so that we could hear what the principal had to say.

"Good morning, children. I trust that we are having a splendid beginning to this school year," Miss Cherrybaum chirped. "Unfortunately, someone has put a dent in our first

LOLO

day of school by pulling a prank. Every poster with a face on it has been given a pair of purple glasses and a beard." All the kids in our class started to snicker. We could even hear kids in other classrooms laughing.

Miss Cherrybaum continued. "If the prankster is caught, he or she will be suspended from school for a week. That is all. Have an excellent first day." Miss Cherrybaum signed off and the PA was quiet. Suspended for a whole week? I figured out quickly that Miss Cherrybaum was for real.

Miss Fuqua looked us up and down.

Then somebody knocked softly at our door. It was Ro. Miss Fuqua answered and let Ro step inside our classroom.

He put on his nice-boy voice. He batted his eyelashes, too. Sometimes he does that to Ma to get out of trouble. It never works.

"Uh . . . excuse me, Miss Fuqua, but I'm Ruby Booker's big brother Roosevelt. Well, um, I'm *one* of her big b-b-brothers," Ro stuttered. That's another one of his tricks. He thinks that people will be nicer to him if he fakes a stutter. "Can I talk to Ruby for a minute? I have something to give her from our mother." Miss Fuqua fell for Ro's act and called me over to the door.

"Ruby, your brother wants to see you," she said. Then she turned to Ro and said, "You've got three minutes, young man. We're about to start our silent reading time."

I stepped into the hall with Ro. When the classroom door shut, the real Ro came out.

"I'm glad she's gone. How's your new teacher? She sure looks mean," Ro said with a silly half frown, half smile on his face. I guess he thinks that makes him look tough.

"Don't talk about my teacher, Ro. She's so nice, and fun, and she has lots of style. I really like her."

"She'll change. I'm sure of that. They all do," Ro said, all tough.

"Shouldn't you be in class, Ro?" I wanted to know.

"I should, but I'm not. My teacher thinks I'm in the nurse's office." He laughed.

"So what do you want? What do you have to give me?" I was getting annoyed with Ro. He took his book bag off, dropped it on the floor, and pulled out a purple marker from it.

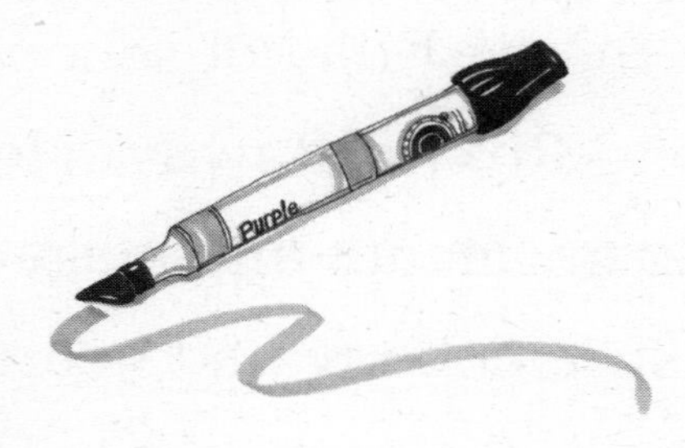

"I need you to keep this for me. Just hide it in your guitar bag, and then give it back to me when we get home, okay?" he asked. I reached for the marker without even asking a question, but then it hit me. This was *the* marker. The purple marker that messed up all of those posters.

"IT WAS YOU! You marked all of those posters, didn't you!" I didn't mean to yell, but it all came together. Who else would've done something so crazy on the first day of school? I'll tell you who — Ro, Ro Rowdy. He put his hand over my mouth and looked around to make sure nobody had heard me.

"Girl, are you nuts? Are you trying to get me busted?" Ro said like a scared rat.

"Is this what you do every year? I see why you get in trouble all of the time. You just can't help it, can you, Ro?"

He looked up toward the ceiling and tapped his chin, then answered, "If it wasn't for me, this place would be boring, Ruby. Besides, some of those ugly posters needed a makeover. All I'm asking you to do is keep this marker for me. Please. I'm going to be the first one Cherrybaum checks today. Help your big bro out," Ro begged.

"Why are you telling me? Why do you want to give the marker to me?" I asked.

"No one will ever think that you, the new girl, the sweet Booker sister, would have anything to do with this," Ro said as he put a hand on my shoulder. "You could save me from getting into trouble, Ruby." He didn't stutter or try his fake sweet-boy routine on me, but I was *not* going to help Ro. He got himself into this mess. He'd have to get himself out.

"No, Ro. Don't put me in the middle," I said. "I have an idea, though. Hold on." While everyone was busy with silent reading time, I slipped quietly back into Pluto-3 and dashed to the sink near the coat closet. I grabbed two sponges and a small spray bottle filled with water and soap. I eased out into the hallway before Miss Fuqua called me to class. "Here." I shoved the sponges and spray bottle into Ro's hands.

"What do you want me to do with this?" Ro asked.

"You're going to clean off those posters. That's what you're going to do. Don't start off your school year like this, Ro."

He still had purple marker stains on his fingertips. But he looked serious, like he was thinking hard about something. "Well, I do have a lot of pranks planned this year. No need to get into trouble so early, I guess. Right?"

"Right." I nodded. I was glad to see Ro change his mind. I sure didn't want to be a part of that purple-marker mess. The only thing was, I never knew what else Ro had up his sleeve.

But he sounded pretty honest when he said, "This should be easy. That purple marker is washable. Those beards and glasses will come off easily." Ro thanked me and then gave me a big hug. I gave him a little punch in the gut. He said, "What was *that* for?"

"I just felt like doing it. Get away from here. And go wash your hands," I said. Ro picked up his book bag and took off down the hallway.

I went back inside Pluto-3 and sat next to Teresa, who was now on the computer.

For the rest of the morning, all the kids in my class kept talking about how funny the purple-marker-poster prank was. When we walked in the hallways on our way to the cafeteria, I could hear kids of all grade levels talking about it. Some kids we passed said that whoever did it was probably the coolest kid in the school. It seemed like everyone was talking about the purple-marker prank in the cafeteria. Even the food servers were chattering about Ro's stunt.

I couldn't help plugging my ears. I might have looked goofy, but at least

I couldn't hear anyone talking about Ro's silly stunt. Later, when the purple marker had been wiped off, nobody would know that I was the one who gave Ro the sponges and soapy water so he could clean the posters. No one would know it was Ruby Booker who saved Ro Rowdy from getting suspended. All they cared about was the purple beards and glasses that caused a big commotion on the first day of school.

I had a feeling that Ro's craziness wouldn't be the only Booker-boy event of the day.

I was right.

6
Big-Time

Even in a lunchroom full of kids, Miss Fuqua saw everything. "Ruby Booker, take your fingers out of your ears," she said from across the cafeteria. "The earrings you have on are cute enough." I took my fingers out quickly. Plus, she was right about how cute my earrings were.

When we went back to Pluto-3, Miss Fuqua said, "Okay, guys, it's Galaxy time."

"What's Galaxy time?" I asked.

"That means that we'll have quiet time, and listen to soft music, and then everyone will do something creative at the different tables around the room."

As soon as Miss Fuqua said *creative*, all I could think of was singing. I wanted to share my singing with my new classmates so badly. "Cotton Candy Clouds" would not stop playing in my head. I had to work hard to keep from singing out as loudly as I'd done that morning.

Teresa went over to the art table and drew a picture of her family. I saw Marquetta Loopy go to the crafts

table, where she made jewelry. Manny Flemon went over to one of the five libraries we have in the room. Low-Low had earphones on. He was listening to who knows what at the music station.

I ran over to Miss Fuqua while she was sitting on the big planet Earth rug in the center of the room.

Music Station
Jazz
Rules For Music Stations
Classical
Pop
R&B
Song Book

She sat cross-legged and was reading a book of poems. I knelt down and whispered to her, "Miss Fuqua? Excuse me. Miss Fuqua, would it be okay if I sang a song to the class for Galaxy time?"

Miss Fuqua looked at me and smiled. She asked me to help her up from the rug. I reached out my hand, and she sprang up like a piece of toast. Miss Fuqua looked excited.

"Sure, Ruby. We'd love to hear you. Please, share your gift." She asked everyone to come around the planet Earth rug so they could hear me. I was so ready to show my classmates how well I can sing. But my hands got all cold and sweaty, and I just couldn't stop flicking my bracelets.

On the planet Earth rug, I stood on the continent of North America, cleared my throat, and then prepared to sing.

But before I could hit one note, the PA system came on for the second time that day. It was the office secretary, Miss Funkhouser. "Pardon the interruption, teachers. But Miss Cherrybaum would like you to please bring your students down to the auditorium in fifteen minutes for a surprise Welcome Back to School assembly. That will be all." Miss Fuqua asked all of us to get in line at the door.

There I was with a song stuck in my throat and standing on North America all by myself.

"We'll continue this some other time,

Ruby," Miss Fuqua called out to me from the door. "Come on now."

I stood in the back of the line and thought about how I might have missed a chance to make a name for myself, at least in my own class. We all walked down the hallway toward the big auditorium.

The curtains on the stage opened all the way. A woman wearing a purple dress came marching out. She looked like a super-sized grape. She was tall, too. Her dress was so pretty. It matched the white-and-purple flower in her hair.

She tapped the microphone twice, then said, "Welcome, students and teachers. I am Miss Cherrybaum, your principal here at Hope Road Academy." Her voice and the way she looked didn't match at all. Her voice was small and squeaky, like a chipmunk's.

Miss Cherrybaum announced, "Please give a warm Hope Road welcome to our music teacher, Mr. Dilla." Mr. Dilla looked so cool. He reminded me of my daddy. He wore glasses and a hat with a feather in it.

A few big kids had set up instruments onstage. It looked like a band was about to play. There was a piano, a saxophone, a flute, and a xylophone.

Suddenly, a beat came through the big speakers in front of the stage, a *boom-cack-ba-boom-cack* kind of beat. Mr. Dilla walked up to the microphone and said, "Okay, Hope Road, I'd like to welcome to the stage my number-one student, a very talented young man who will open up our assembly. Keep the beat going for my one-man band . . . MARCELLUS BOOKER!"

My chance to sing in front of my class had been cut short because of my brother Marcellus. I couldn't believe it! And now he was going to be a big fat show-off in front of the whole

school. Great. I could feel a frown pinching my face. My lips were as tight as a zipper. I balled my fists up like I was getting ready for a boxing match.

Whenever company came over to our house, Daddy always had

Marcellus and me perform together. He played the piano, and I hit all of the notes. I wanted to go up on that stage with Marcellus to sing, sing, sing. "Cotton Candy Clouds" would have sounded so good with Marcellus playing the piano. But I had to stay in my seat while Marcellus strolled onto the stage by himself. He clapped with the crowd and then took a seat at the piano. He smiled at everyone and began to play.

Then Marcellus got up from the piano and grabbed the saxophone. He played for a few minutes. It sounded as smooth as butter. Then he grabbed the flute and played it so sweetly.

While still playing the flute, Marcellus walked over to the xylophone. He handed the flute to Mr. Dilla. Then my super-talented big bro tapped the xylophone with little soft hammer-looking things. It was amazing!

A few rows back from me, a boy stood up and hollered out, "Sit down, show-off!" I think he was a fifth- or sixth-grader. It didn't matter to me what the kid thought. Marcellus may have been showing off, but he was *good* at it.

I stood on my seat and then turned around to face the boy who yelled out. He looked really surprised and a little scared at the mean face I gave him. I rolled up my sleeves and pointed at him.

"If you don't mind, some people are enjoying this. Keep your mean, silly words to yourself," I growled at him. I also cracked my knuckles like Ro does when he's trying to bully me into doing something for him. My knuckles don't make that cracking sound like Ro's do, but my rolled-up sleeves were enough. That boy slid down in his seat and kept his mouth shut for the rest of the assembly.

After the assembly was over, all of the classes went back to their rooms. In the hallways, *again* I heard everyone talking about one of my brothers. Marcellus "Big-Time" Booker was the star this time. Everyone thought it was so cool how he could play all of those instruments. Well . . . it *was* a big deal, but I didn't want to hear it.

When we returned to our classroom, I put my head down on my desk and waited for Miss Fuqua to pass out our math books. I was eager for the day to end.

There was *no way* Tyner would show me up. At least I hoped he wouldn't.

7
Ty Noodles

I didn't get to sing during Galaxy time, but when it was math time, I knew this could be my time to shine. I was always good at math. I like it. To tell you the truth, it's always been fun for me. Tyner has taught me math. And since *all* subjects are easy for Tyner, when he shows me stuff, he makes it seem easy.

"Would any of you brave souls like to come up to the board and try a few math problems?" Miss Fuqua asked as she waved a piece of chalk.

My hand was the first one in the air. I even stood up.

"Right here, Miss Fuqua!"

I ran to the board, grabbed the chalk from Miss Fuqua, and wrote down five problems that Miss Fuqua read from a book on her desk. She wanted to see how fast I could find the answers. It didn't take me long at all. I zoomed through those problems.

One thing that always helped me keep calm while doing math was humming. So as soon as I got to that blackboard, another song by the Crazy Cutie Crew called "Jelly Bean

Dreams" came into my head. While I was writing down each number I sang softly to myself. I don't think anyone could hear me:

"Jelly, jelly, jelly,
Rolling in my belly.
Purple, green, orange, and red.
Jelly, jelly, jelly, that's what I said!"

Maybe Miss Fuqua heard a little, but she didn't mind. I think she was more into my math skills. I wrote quickly, with a steady hand. I showed the kids in Pluto-3 that I really meant business.

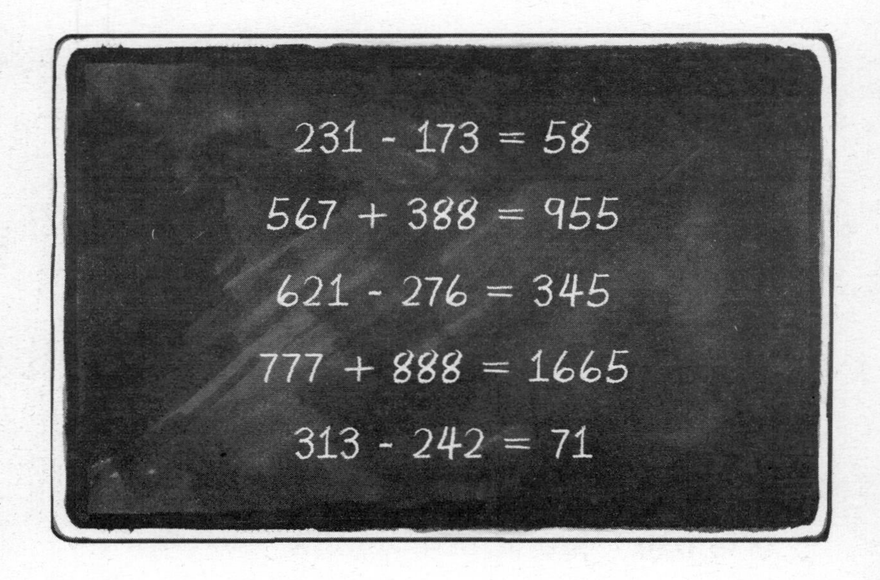

Miss Fuqua clapped at my speedy answers. I bowed like I'd just won a big contest. The look on some of my classmates' faces made me feel proud. Even they couldn't believe how good I was at math. Only one girl had a frown on her face. It was Marquetta Loopy, of course. I didn't let her ruin my happy moment, though. I stood proudly by my work.

But then — *aargh!* — just like the other times during the day, the PA system came on . . . *again*. It was our school counselor, Mrs. Prize.

"Close your math books, everyone. I need you to listen," Miss Fuqua told the class. Then she turned to me and said, "Good job, Ruby. Have a seat, please."

Mrs. Prize began to speak. "Students, your grades are a reflection of your efforts. We hope you'll have a great year and be the best students and leaders that you can be." Mrs. Prize kept reading off numbers and grades of students from Hope Road Academy who did well last year. She also mentioned how Miss Cherrybaum wants those students to set good examples and to keep up the good work.

Mrs. Prize finished her list and then started to go on and on about the best student at Hope Road. I didn't even need to guess who she was talking about. I was just hoping that it wasn't who I thought it was . . . but it was.

Mrs. Prize said, "But the student with the highest grades and test scores by far is none other than Tyner Booker."

There is a sixth-grade classroom above Pluto-3, and we could hear them cheering and stomping for Tyner. Mrs. Prize read off Tyner's perfect scores, and the kids in my class were amazed. It seemed like my three-digit subtraction and addition stuff didn't even matter anymore.

I know that it wasn't Ty's fault, but now he had outshined me, too. I was as low as low could ever go. My legs felt like pudding, my nose started to run, and I walked back to my desk and slumped down like an old beanbag.

Miss Fuqua said it was time for us to go out for recess. If anybody needed a break, it was me.

8
Waiting on a Good Turn

Teresa and I were the only girls who wanted to play kick ball. We leaned against the fence, just waiting on our turn to kick. Until then, we munched on the sunflower seeds that she'd brought. That girl *loves* sunflower seeds. Between spitting out the shells, I told her how low I felt about my brothers stealing all of the Booker attention away from me.

"I hear ya, Ruby," Teresa said.

"You don't have any brothers or

sisters, T. How could you understand?" I asked after I dug deeper into her pocket for more seeds.

"I *do* understand, Ruby," Teresa said. "I have some big cousins back home, and they're always beating me at *something*."

"Yeah, but you don't have to share anything, fight with anyone, or compete with anyone at home."

"That's true, but it sure would be nice to have someone to play with, even fight and compete with from time to time. You're lucky, gal!" Teresa said before she chipped away at more sunflower seeds.

"I know, T, but it can be annoying sometimes. Marcellus is good at everything, Ty is a brainiac, and even though Ro acts up, he's famous for his pranks."

"You do have some awesome brothers, Ruby, but you're no choppy livers yourself."

"I'm no *what*?" Sometimes I don't know what that country girl is talking about.

"My dad says that every now and then. It means that you're good at a lot of things, but maybe you don't know it sometimes. Like singing. You sing like a bird, Ruby. Those Booker boys can't sing like you do." Teresa was right.

We moved up a couple of spaces in the kick-ball line. There were four boys ahead of me. I thought Teresa and I would never get a turn to kick the ball.

"I know that, but how can I get everybody here at Hope Road to know me if I keep getting shoved to the back?" I said to Teresa. "People don't even call me by my name in the neighborhood. They say, 'Hey! Aren't you Ty, Ro, and Big-Time's little sis?' I'm so sick of that! I didn't come to this school to hear about how great my brothers are." I pouted like I almost never do. My cheeks got all puffy and I folded my arms.

"I know how fun you are, Ruby, and how well you can carry a tune," Teresa said in her sweet-peach voice. "Who else could dress as fancy as you do or wear her hair in such a stylish way and still look cuter than a baby possum in an Easter basket? You, that's who." Teresa shook more sunflower seeds into her hand, popped one into the air, and then caught it with her mouth.

"So what should I do? How can I get my name in lights here at this giant school?" I asked Teresa. There were two more kids in front of me. I wasn't keeping up with the score, but our team was kicking tail!

"I really don't know," she said. Then she turned her lips up and looked toward the sky. That's what she does when her brain is clicking. Then she said, "I got it! What did you do this morning to get yourself ready to come to Hope Road? I know morning time is always a happy time for you. What did you do?"

"You know . . . I woke up singing my favorite song."

"'Cotton Candy Clouds'?"

"What else?" I answered. We looked at each other and started singing the words:

"When the sun hits the clouds
And rainbows kiss the sky,
A sweet wind blows, and then I know
That today is mine, all mine."

We sang it over and over. Teresa was not the greatest singer in the world, but I wouldn't have chosen anyone else as a singing buddy. Her peach-cake twang sounded so cool to me. Besides, she was trying to make me feel better, and I love that about her.

Right then, an idea hit me. It was as sweet as the cotton candy clouds over our heads. Yeah, I *could* sing for the whole school. And my brothers or Miss Fuqua wouldn't be able to stop me. I didn't tell Teresa my secret plan. I just hoped I would get a chance to do it before the day was over. I knew what I had to do. I was ready.

When Teresa saw me grinning, she said, "There's that famous glowworm Ruby smile that I'm used to!" She nudged me up toward home plate. It was my turn to kick.

A boy from the other third-grade class laughed and told the kids on

his team to move closer because he didn't think I could kick. *Well*, I tricked his treat.

As soon as that bouncy red ball rolled over the plate, I slammed it with my purple sneaker. I could see the eyes of all the boys on that other team get as big as lightbulbs. The ball flew over their heads and would have been a home run if there'd been a wall for it to fly over. I smashed it! Then I went around the bases real slow and waved at all the boys who didn't believe in my kick-ball skills.

9
My Mic Sounds Nice

We had thirty minutes left before the bell rang for us to go home. Miss Fuqua asked the class, "Could you please clean up around your desks?" My area was clean. Manny Flemon had crayons, cut-up strips of paper, and glue balls that looked like boogers stuck to his desk.

When we finished, we went to the coat closet and grabbed our things, one group at a time. Then Miss Fuqua surprised us, especially me, when she stood before the class and said, "Pluto-3 has been given the honor of selecting a student to go to the office and read the first-day-of-school announcements."

I crossed my fingers, closed my eyes to make a wish, and tried hard not to blurt out, "Me, me, me!" But Miss Fuqua kept looking at Marquetta Loopy, like she'd been chosen. I just kept wishing. *Me. Me. Me.* And, yeah! My wish came true. Miss Fuqua walked past grumpy-faced Marquetta Loopy and came right over to me. "You'll be first, Ruby Booker. You've been such a good leader and such an interesting new member of Pluto-3. Make us proud."

This was my turn to shine! *Me. Me. Me.* The plan I thought up to finally get everyone's attention could happen now. This was so perfect. I smiled at Marquetta, even though she was still frowning.

Miss Fuqua said I could come back later to get my stuff from the classroom. She said reading the announcements would only take about three minutes. I grabbed the hall pass from a hook by the door and tore down the hall like a jet-powered kid.

I went down the steps, and there was Miss Cherrybaum fussing, in her high, squeaky, chipmunk voice, at some boy who had been caught running down the stairs, throwing pieces of paper off the banister.

When I walked past Miss Cherrybaum and the goofy-looking boy who got caught, Miss Cherrybaum stopped me and said, "I'm counting on you to do a good job with those announcements, Miss Ruby Booker." Miss Cherrybaum smiled at me and then turned back to the boy. The flower that she had in her hair from the assembly was still there. Now that I was up close, I could see that it was real.

"Your flower is pretty, Miss Cherrybaum. It looks good on you," I told her. She looked at me again and smiled even wider. She told me to go into her office and wait for her to come in. So that's what I did. No one was in the office at the time. Even the secretary, Miss Funkhouser, had stepped out for a break.

When I walked into Miss Cherrybaum's office, the first thing I noticed was the big golden microphone for the PA system sitting on her desk. That was the same microphone that kept interrupting my moments of greatness all day. The announcements were written on a piece of paper on her desk. They looked short and sweet. The button to turn on the microphone was calling my name. All I had to do was flick it on when the time came.

I thought that maybe Miss Cherrybaum would think it was very leader-like to read the announcements without being told. But really, the announcements were the last thing on my mind. I thought that maybe it was my turn to flip the switch and introduce myself to the whole school. But then I stopped myself. *What are you doing, Ruby Booker!?* I thought.

I started to walk out of Miss Cherrybaum's office when the words to "Cotton Candy Clouds" came over me. This was the right moment to jump on!

There was the microphone. And there *I* stood, ready to share with the whole school who the real Ruby Booker was. I shut the door to the office, but I didn't lock it. I walked back over to the desk, turned on the microphone, and took a deep, deep breath.

"Good afternoon, Hope Road. This is Ruby Booker from Miss Fuqua's third-grade class." I was a little nervous, too. I wanted to say my name but not say anything about my brothers. This was about *me*, not them. I continued, "Instead of reading the announcements, I want to do something different. Here we go."

And then . . . I sang. I sang loud. I sang strong. I sang for the whole school to hear:

"When the sun hits the clouds
And rainbows kiss the sky,
A sweet wind blows, and then I know
That today is mine, all mine."

I knew that most of the kids, especially the girls, were fans of the Crazy Cutie Crew, so I could almost see the kids sitting at their seats and singing the words along with me. Through the walls, I could even hear kids from the classrooms next to the office singing. How cool was *that*?!

Nobody told me to sing. I just did it. I knew I was probably going to get in trouble for singing over the PA system, but it just seemed like the right time to shine. When I finished singing "*today is mine, all mine*" for the second time, Miss Cherrybaum came rushing through the door and then shut it behind her. I switched the microphone off after I told the entire school, "Let's have a good school year, y'all." The wide smile Miss Cherrybaum had given me in the hallway had gone away. Miss Cherrybaum pointed at the seat in front of her desk. That meant for me to sit down. So I did.

Miss Cherrybaum came over to her seat behind the desk. She stared at me over the golden microphone. I just knew I would be in so much trouble. *What made me do something so dumb?*

All of a sudden, Miss Cherrybaum broke into a smile and said, chipmunk-style, "Ruby Booker, THAT WAS GREAT!"

"What? I mean . . . what do you mean?" I asked Miss Cherrybaum.

"That was the most colorful, well-prepared yet unexpected school announcement I've ever heard. Your voice is beautiful!"

I just sat there blinking.

"Ruby Booker, you can come back to sing and read the announcements anytime!" Miss Cherrybaum squeaked.

She also said that my voice reminded her of Ella Fitzgerald's, a famous singer from the old days. That was probably a compliment.

Even if every kid in the school still didn't know who I was, they would never forget the voice that floated out of the speakers into their classrooms. One thing was for sure. I knew three boys in this school who would now have to see me as an equal Booker. As long as they knew that I would be as big a Booker as they were at Hope Road Academy, that's all that mattered to me.

When I walked back into Pluto-3,

Miss Fuqua and the rest of my classmates gave me a standing ovation. Even Marquetta Loopy was standing.

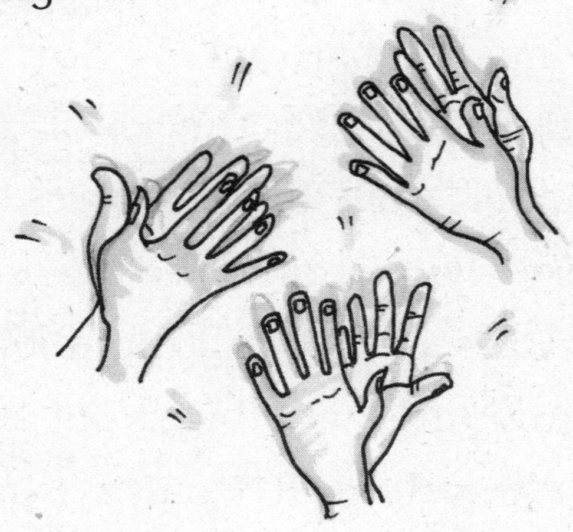

10
Hanging with the Boys

From my classroom . . . down the stairs that lead to the door out of the school . . . out on the blacktop . . . and everywhere around the buses . . . all I heard were people talking about that "cool Ruby girl" who burst out singing on the PA system. It wouldn't be long before everyone knew *I* was that "cool Ruby girl."

I met my brothers at the front gates of the school grounds. They stood there, looking at me with their arms folded.

They couldn't believe what I had done. But they didn't say one word, not even Ro. Out of all the stunts and pranks he'd pulled, he would never be able to top what I did. Ever. Even though Ro's a prankster, he can't sing half as good as me. Same with Marcellus, who hates it when anyone else does something he can't do. And Tyner probably just couldn't believe what his baby sis found the courage to do.

All of us Bookers walked down Hope Road. We turned on the corner of Fifty-fifth Street and passed Marcellus's favorite malt shop, Joe Milky's Place. We hit Chill Brook Avenue and saw the

big boys playing basketball in Freedom Park. We made it to our brownstone in no time flat. And for the whole walk home, not one Booker boy said a peep to me. But they *were* smiling and giving me the Booker bump with their elbows. Ro and Marcellus climbed the stairs to our house and went inside. I sat on our stoop, and Tyner began to walk in, too. He stopped halfway up the steps, came back down, and sat next to me.

"I knew you could do it," he said, then put an arm around my shoulders. I looked at him and smiled. "All our school needed was a little Ruby Booker flavor, and I'm glad you're there." He gave me a pound of Booker, like Daddy does to them, and then ran into the house.

I went in to get my pet iguana, Lady Love, and we came back out on the stoop. I wanted to take in the sunshine, watch the people walk past, and say hey to everyone who knew me. Most of all, I wanted to think about how good it felt to finally be on my way to becoming my own Booker.

☆ Ruby's Laptop Journal ☆

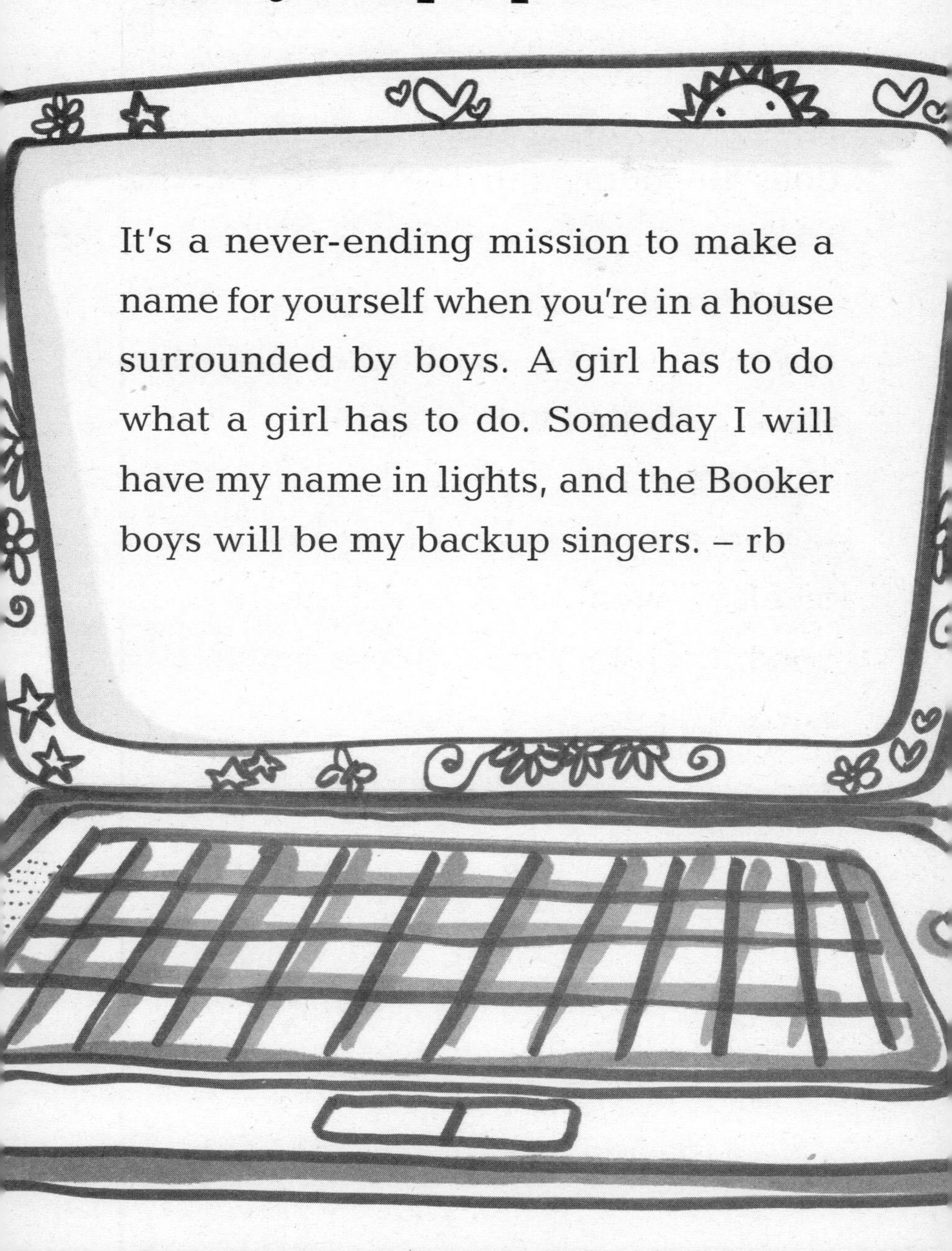

It's a never-ending mission to make a name for yourself when you're in a house surrounded by boys. A girl has to do what a girl has to do. Someday I will have my name in lights, and the Booker boys will be my backup singers. – rb

☆ Get set for Ruby's next ☆ adventure, when she takes the spotlight (well, that's the plan, anyway . . .)

If you know anything about Ruby Booker, you know she's ready to make a name for herself. Well, her chance is coming up: There's an animal trivia contest, and the winner gets season passes to the Chill Brook Zoo—for everyone in their grade!

The problem is, Ruby needs a little help. And for her entire life, help has come in the shape of Marcellus,

Roosevelt, and Tyner. This time around, for the first time ever, she'll have to face two of them. They're older, they're popular, and they've each got their own thing. But so does Ruby. And she's about to show it to the world.

Read *Trivia Queen, 3rd Grade Supreme* to find out how Ruby gets the chance of a lifetime.

☆ About the Author ☆

Derrick Barnes is the author of the series Ruby and the Booker Boys: *Brand-new School, Brave New Ruby* and *Trivia Queen, 3rd Grade Supreme.* He's also written *Stop, Drop, and Chill* and *Low-down Bad Day Blues* as well as books for young adults. He is a native of Kansas City, Missouri, although he spent a good portion of his formative years in Mississippi. A graduate of Jackson State University, he has written bestselling copy for various Hallmark Cards lines and was the first African-American male staff writer for Hallmark. Derrick and his wife, Tinka, reside in Kansas City with their own version of the Booker boys — Ezra, Solomon, and Silas.